The
Lighthouse
Keeper's Rescue

Once upon a time there
was a lighthouse keeper called
Mr Grinling. He lived with
Mrs Grinling and their cat,
Hamish, in a little white cottage
on the cliffs.

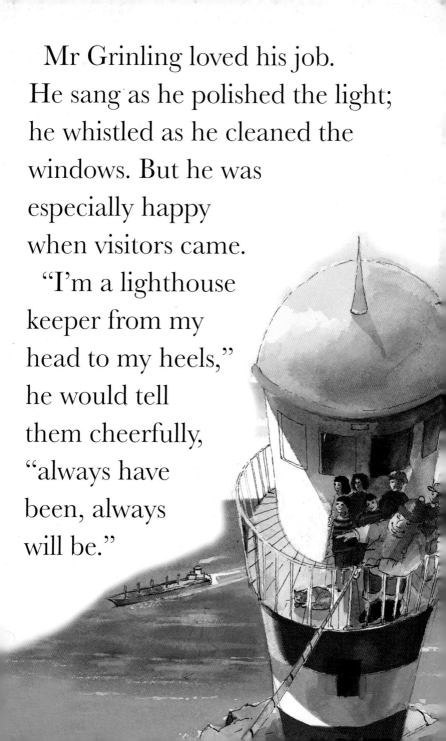

Mr Grinling loved his job.
He sang as he polished the light;
he whistled as he cleaned the
windows. But he was
especially happy
when visitors came.

"I'm a lighthouse
keeper from my
head to my heels,"
he would tell
them cheerfully,
"always have
been, always
will be."

He was also a lighthouse keeper who was getting old. Sometimes he could hear his bones creaking as he climbed the lighthouse stairs.

One day Mrs Grinling found him by the shed, dozing with his head under a heliotrope. She woke him gently.

"What's the matter, Mr G?" she asked anxiously. "Are you ill?"

"No, Mrs G," said Mr Grinling, politely. "I'm just having a little snooze in the sun."

But all was not well. One afternoon Mr Grinling and Hamish rowed out to the lighthouse to prepare the night light. Mr Grinling was tired after rowing so he decided to have a nap. When he awoke it was dark.

"Oh those poor boats!" he exclaimed as he rushed into the lighthouse. "I do hope there hasn't been an accident," and he peered anxiously into the darkness.

There hadn't been an accident, but somebody had noticed that the light had not come on.

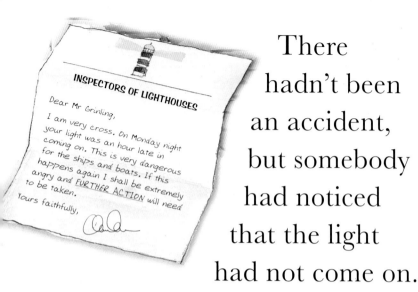

INSPECTORS OF LIGHTHOUSES

Dear Mr Grinling,

I am very cross. On Monday night your light was an hour late in coming on. This is very dangerous for the ships and boats. If this happens again I shall be extremely angry and FURTHER ACTION will need to be taken.

Yours faithfully,

A few days later Mr Grinling received a letter from the inspector of lighthouses.

For a while Mr Grinling made sure he didn't fall asleep anywhere except in his bed. He was careful not to doze by the shed and he certainly didn't rest his head underneath the heliotrope flowers.

One sunny afternoon as he was on his way to the lighthouse, Mr Grinling stopped to watch three squabbling seagulls. The dinghy rocked gently up and down. Mr Grinling closed his eyes, leaned back and soon fell fast asleep.

The dinghy dipped gently in and out of the waves until it was far beyond the lighthouse.

When the light didn't come on, Mrs Grinling began to worry. She rang the coastguard.

"Don't fret, love," he said, "I'll send the launch out straight away. We'll soon find him. He's probably gone to sleep again."

But Mr Grinling found the coastguard first. The crunching noise as the dinghy hit the launch woke him. For a moment he was very frightened. The coastguard shouted to him.

"At last! Hold tight and we'll tow you to the lighthouse. With luck you might get the light on before anybody notices."

But Mr Grinling was not lucky. The next day three inspectors of lighthouses arrived at the little white cottage. They wore grey suits and long faces.

"We are extremely cross, Mr Grinling," they said. "You cannot keep falling asleep, it isn't right for a lighthouse keeper.

"We must take FURTHER ACTION. You have always been a good and conscientious lighthouse keeper, but now you need to rest. We have given your job to a younger man. Goodbye, Mr Grinling."

They shook his hand, took the lighthouse key and left.

Mr Grinling was so upset that he went straight to bed.

Nothing that Mrs Grinling did would comfort him. She cooked his favourite breakfast and his favourite dinner. She sang him *'Humpty Dumpty'* – his favourite song – but Mr Grinling didn't stir. He just lay there staring at the ceiling.

After a week Mrs Grinling decided she'd had enough.

"Mr G," she said sternly, "I've had enough. You can't lie in bed forever. I need you to help me pack. Now stop this nonsense at once."

So Mr Grinling climbed out of bed and together he and Mrs Grinling packed their trunk. From time to time a tear would roll down Mr Grinling's cheek.

"Whatever shall I do, Mrs G?" he asked sadly. "I'm a lighthouse keeper. I don't know how to do anything else."

They were very
tired when
they finished
packing, but
Mrs Grinling said she wanted a
last look through the telescope.

"Whatever's that?" she exclaimed. "There's an enormous black shape on the beach, Mr G. We must find out what it is."

Together they ran down the steep, winding path to the beach below.

And then they stopped. There it lay on the sand, a great black, shiny whale.

"Jiminy Cricket!" exclaimed Mr Grinling. "It's a whale. He must have got lost. We can't leave him here, Mrs G. If he stays out of the water he will die."

"We won't let him die," said Mrs Grinling firmly. "I'll just consult my book." And she did.

"We will need help to push him, Mr G," she decided. "You must ride to the village and bring back as many people as you can find. At 3 o'clock it will be high tide. We might be able to float him then."

"While you're away, I shall throw water over him to keep him cool and I shall talk to him so he doesn't feel lonely."

Away went Mr Grinling as fast
as his fat little legs could pedal.

All the villagers came.
The butcher, the baker, the
electrician, the schoolchildren
and their teachers, the grannies
and the granddads.

Some of them ran out of breath
and were left behind.

"Hurry!" shouted Mrs Grinling as she saw them coming. "The water's right in now and it's time to push."

Everybody gathered round the whale.

"Ready, steady, push!" called
Mr Grinling. They pushed and
shoved and huffed and puffed
until everybody was purple in the
face. But the whale WAS moving.
Slowly the water crept up his big,
shiny sides until he was floating.

Everybody stopped pushing
and watched.

The whale looked at them, then
with a flick of his enormous
black tail, he turned and
headed out to sea.

"Goodbye!" called the
villagers. "Good luck!"

That evening the villagers and the Grinlings watched the whale rescue on the television news.

"It will soon be time for us to say goodbye," said Mrs Grinling. "Tomorrow we have to leave the little white cottage on the cliff. But before we go we'll have a farewell picnic. And we would like you all to come."

Everybody came. The butcher, the baker and the electrician, the children on their bikes and the babies in their pushchairs.

It was a very
merry affair.
Then three guests
turned up, who had
not been invited.

"We saw you on the television
news," explained the first inspector.

"Yes," said the second inspector,
"we were so proud of you and
Mrs Grinling."

"We want you to be the
lighthouse keeper again," said
the third inspector, "but we will
give you an assistant. You will
work on Mondays, Wednesdays
and Fridays and he'll do the rest
of the week."

Mr and Mrs Grinling were so delighted that they jumped up and down for joy.

"Three cheers for the inspectors of lighthouses," shouted the villagers, "and three cheers for the Grinlings!"

The Lighthouse Keeper's Catastrophe

Mr Grinling was a lighthouse keeper. He lived with Mrs Grinling in a little white cottage on the cliffs. Every morning he rowed out to his lighthouse to clean and polish the light.

Every morning Mrs Grinling
prepared a delicious lunch for
him. At lunch time Mrs Grinling
packed the lunch in a basket
and sent it down the wire to
the lighthouse.

On high days and holidays when the sun shone Mr and Mrs Grinling opened up the lighthouse, hung the key safely on its hook inside and spent many contented hours fishing.

Hamish the cat lazed about in the sun. From time to time he roused himself to chase the seagulls.

This particular morning chasing seagulls was not what Hamish had in mind. He was much too busy enjoying himself in other ways.

Mr Grinling was not at all pleased when he saw what Hamish was doing.

"Move it, pussy cat," he snarled as he chased Hamish into the lighthouse. "That'll teach you to steal our fish, you little varmint," and without thinking he slammed the door shut.

 Mr and
Mrs Grinling
continued with
their fishing. Soon,
Mr Grinling's
stomach reminded
him that lunch would be very
welcome. As he went to let
Hamish out he was struck by
a terrible thought. The key, where
was the lighthouse door key?
Of course, it was inside.

Mr Grinling did his very best to get Hamish out of the lighthouse. He rattled the lock as hard as he could. He pushed, he kicked and he cursed, but the door stayed firmly shut.

"Don't worry," soothed Mrs Grinling, "Hamish is quite safe where he is. We have the spare key in the old teapot on the mantelpiece in the kitchen."

The spare key was exactly where
Mrs Grinling said it would be –
in the teapot. While she prepared
cold chicken sandwiches, a fruit
salad with lots of strawberries
and a chocolate milkshake for his
lunch, Mr Grinling listened to
the midday weather forecast. It
was perfectly dreadful. Wind and
rain with possible thunder and
lightening later in the day.

"I don't like the sound of that weather, Mrs G," said Mr Grinling. "The sooner I get back to the lighthouse, rescue Hamish and switch on the light, the happier I shall be. If you could pack the lunch in the basket I'll take it with me. Remind me to take a screwdriver, Mrs G. I have some repair work to do."

So Mr Grinling set off down the steep, winding path with his lunch and the key in the lunch basket.

It was not until he was halfway down the hill that he heard Mrs Grinling calling from the little white cottage.

"The screwdriver, Mr G, you've forgotten the screwdriver."

"Botheration," he muttered. Climbing cliff paths for a plump lighthouse keeper was rather hard work. He put the lunch basket on the bank and stomped back towards the house.

Oh what a silly man, he really ought to have known better. Already the seagulls were beginning to gather. As he turned the corner…

…down they swooped. Such greedy creatures. They squabbled and flapped and squawked and tugged, trying to get to the lunch. Finally the basket started to move. Down the slope it went, tumbling, bumping, faster and faster, over and over and over until it came to the cliff edge. For a moment it almost seemed to stop and then…

it was gone.

And so was the key! Down it
drifted, down past the eagle ray
and the angel fish to the seabed.

There it lay amongst the rocks and the seaweed where only the octopus, the crab and other sea creatures would ever find it again.

Mr Grinling was very puzzled upon his return. It was not until Mrs Grinling came to help him search that she found the bits of cold chicken and the odd strawberry. But no lighthouse key – not on the slope – not anywhere.

"Oh, you are a foolish man, Mr G," she exclaimed. "All your life you've lived amongst seagulls and still you leave your lunch for them to eat."

Mr Grinling smiled rather foolishly.

"I'm sure we have a third key somewhere." Mrs Grinling shook her head.

"I don't think so," she said. "Don't you remember, one dropped through the hole in your trousers last year?"

Already the sky was beginning to fill with clouds.

"Well, there's nothing for it, Mr G," said Mrs Grinling. "You'll just have to climb in." So they collected the ladder and rowed back to the lighthouse.

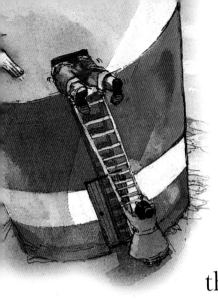

While Mrs Grinling held the ladder, Mr Grinling climbed very slowly to the top.

"I don't like this, Mrs G," he called, "you know I get dizzy when I climb up high."

"Don't look down," she replied, "think of Hamish, think of the light, think of all those poor ships that might be wrecked unless that light shines tonight." But in the end it was not dizziness that stopped Mr Grinling.

Oh, dearie me, no. It was all those scrumptious lunches he had eaten. In through the window he climbed and there he stuck fast. Neither backwards nor forwards could he go – he was just too fat.

Nor could Mrs Grinling help him. She pushed and she pulled and pulled and pushed until he squealed but she couldn't get him to move.

"I'm sorry, Mr G," she said, "there's only one thing to be done – I'll have to remove those great heavy trousers."

Off came the boots and off came the trousers. Mr Grinling wriggled again and at last he was free.

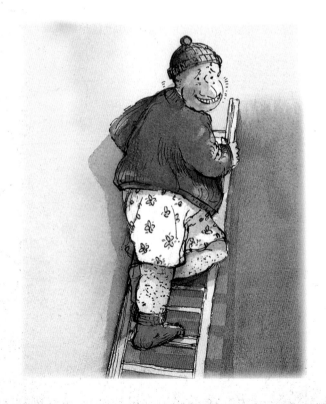

Rowing home was difficult for Mr and Mrs Grinling. The wind was almost gale force by now and the waves kept breaking over the bow of the little boat.

"There must be another key somewhere," said Mr Grinling. "We'll just have to search until we find it."

And search they did. They opened old tins and jars, they emptied out drawers and they peered into cupboards but to no avail – no key labelled LIGHTHOUSE could be found.

Cottage door key (back)

Blue suitcase key

Old key from a wrecked ship

"I'll just have to cycle into the village and alert the coastguards," said Mr Grinling.

"No time," said Mrs Grinling. "Look at that sky. You'll never get there before dark and you haven't got a light on your bike. But I've got an idea — a perfectly brilliant idea."

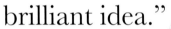
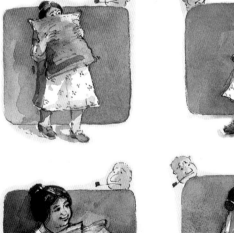

While Mr Grinling looked on, Mrs Grinling rushed about the little white cottage gathering up all manner of things. She put everything she had collected into a large sack.

She weighed the sack and then she weighed Mr Grinling. Mr Grinling began to feel nervous but he wasn't quite sure why.

By the time Mrs Grinling had
attached the sack to the pulley
and sent it down the wire,
Mr Grinling was biting his
fingernails and muttering
to himself.

Mrs Grinling smiled happily. "That worked perfectly," she said. "Your turn now."

Mr Grinling's legs became quite wobbly and he had to sit down quickly in the chair.

"Me," he squeaked, "on that wire – all the way to the lighthouse? You know I am terrified of thunder and lightning, Mrs Grinling. How could you suggest such an idea on a night like this?"

Mrs Grinling spoke to him in a stern voice.

"You must be very brave, Mr Grinling. Think of your poor little Hamish, all alone in the dark. Think of all the ships that might be lost because your light isn't shining." Mr Grinling shuddered.

"Of course you're quite right, Mrs Grinling, I must be brave. I am the lighthouse keeper and come rain or shine I must tend that light."

Without further ado,
Mr Grinling climbed into his
wet weather gear, fastened the
harness around himself and
attached it to the pulley.

A quick glance back at his comfortable armchair, a big kiss of luck from Mrs Grinling, and out he swung into the dark, wet night.

Mrs Grinling watched until
Mr Grinling became a tiny speck
in the darkness. The minutes
ticked by and nothing happened.

Mrs Grinling became quite agitated; why was it taking so long? Had something happened to Mr Grinling?

At last she was able to uncross her fingers and smile again. Her plan had worked! Mr Grinling and Hamish were safe. For there it was for all the ships to see – the light shining steadily and bravely across the ocean.